Tig and Tag

BENEDICT BLATHWAYT

TACKLE & BOOKS

TOBERMORY

One cold night at Bay Farm,
three little lambs were born.

The mother sheep had only enough milk for one lamb,
so the farmer's wife looked after the other two.

The farmhouse became home to them.

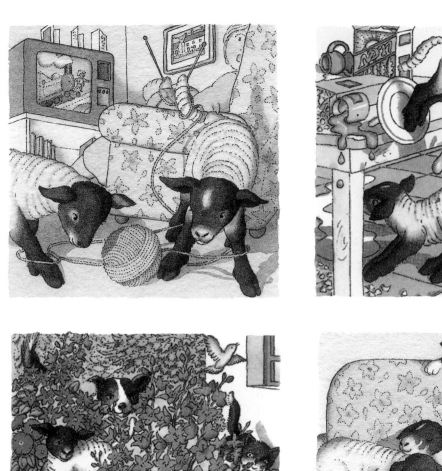

She called the lambs Tig and Tag.

When they grew bigger, Tig and Tag were put
out in the fields with the other sheep.

But they liked the farmhouse better and
kept trying to find a way back.

'You must go and mix with the other sheep,' said the farmer's wife.

But Tig and Tag would not.

Instead they went exploring in the hills . . .

. . . or visited the village.

They got into trouble . . .

. . . and then more trouble.

'You are very naughty sheep,' the farmer's wife
said crossly. 'Please, no more trouble!'

One day lots of people were invited to a party at Bay Farm.
Tig and Tag heard music and laughter in the barn.

One of the guests let her dog out of the car
for some fresh air and a run around.

But the dog ran off and began to chase the sheep.

Tig and Tag watched the bad dog. The sheep were very frightened.

But Tig and Tag were not afraid. They chased the dog out of the field . . .

. . . across the farmyard and into the barn.

Tig and Tag made a terrible mess.

'Oh, you naughty sheep!' cried the farmer's wife.

'But they're not naughty!' cried the dog's owner. 'My dog was to blame.' Tig and Tag were forgiven, and everyone said they were the best and bravest sheep in the world.

But although Tig and Tag had been clever and brave, they
were still always in trouble. One very hot day they heard
the farmer and his dog coming up the hill.

Tig and Tag hid. They didn't want to be rounded up.
It was nice and cool on the hill.

But the sheepdog found them,

and the farmer drove them home to be
sheared with all the other sheep.

The sheep would be cooler without
their thick woollen fleeces.

Tig and Tag watched and waited. They hated being
sheared and soon it would be their turn.

So they climbed over the wall . . .

. . . escaped through the garden . . .

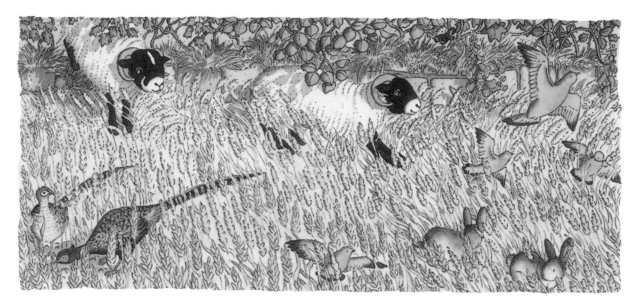

. . . and ran down the edge of the wheat field
until they came to the shore.

The tide was very low and Tig followed
Tag along a narrow strip of sand.

Then the tide came in again.

At first Tig and Tag were very happy on their little island.

But there wasn't much shade and they began to feel very uncomfortable in their heavy woollen coats.

Tig and Tag were miserable. They wanted to go home.

They swam all the way back to Bay Farm.

Tig and Tag were very tired by the time they reached the shore.

'Where have you been?' asked the farmer's wife.
'Let's get those hot, wet fleeces off you.'

Tig and Tag were much more comfortable without their thick
coats. 'You are such naughty sheep,' sighed the farmer's wife.
But she was very pleased to have them safely home.

For Marina

First published in
Great Britain in 2015 by
BC Books an imprint of
Birlinn Ltd
West Newington House
10 Newington Road
Edinburgh EH9 1QS

www.birlinn.co.uk

in association with

Tackle and Books
6–8 Main Street, Tobermory
Isle of Mull PA75 6NU

www.tackleandbooks.co.uk

First published as *Tig and Tag in Trouble* and
Tig and Tag's Island by Julia MacRae Books in 1992

ISBN: 978 1 78027 312 9

British Library Cataloguing-in-Publication Data
A catalogue record for this book is available from the British Library

Designed by Mark Blackadder

Printed and bound by Livonia, Latvia